THE DOODLES OF SAM DIBBLE

Abra-Ca-Doodle!

THE DOODLES OF SAM DIBBLE

OF SAM DIBBLE

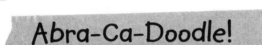

Abra-Ca-Doodle!

by J. Press
illustrated by Michael Kline

Grosset & Dunlap
An Imprint of Penguin Group (USA) LLC

GROSSET & DUNLAP
Published by the Penguin Group
Penguin Group (USA) LLC
375 Hudson Street
New York, New York 10014, USA

USA I Canada I UK I Ireland I Australia I New Zealand I India I South Africa I China

penguin.com
A Penguin Random House Company

Designed by Debbie Guy-Christiansen

Text copyright © 2013 by Judy Press. Illustrations copyright © 2013 by Michael Kline. Published by Grosset & Dunlap, a division of Penguin Young Readers Group, 345 Hudson Street, New York, New York 10014. GROSSET & DUNLAP is a trademark of Penguin Group (USA) LLC. Printed in the U.S.A.

Library of Congress Cataloging-in-Publication Data is available.

ISBN 978-0-448-46110-6   10 9 8 7 6 5 4 3 2 1

For Deb-a-la, my one and only—JP

For the third, fourth, and fifth grades of Roosevelt Elementary in McPherson, Kansas. Ewe guise rawk!—MK

Chapter One
A Recycled Doodle

My name is Sam Dibble. I can sneeze with my eyes open, shoot peas through a straw, and raise just one eyebrow. But what I like to do most is doodle.

I think doodling is a lot of fun. It's like

taking your pen for a walk and going someplace
you've never been before.

I go to Colfax Elementary School, and my
teacher's name is Mrs. Hennessey.

She has laser eyes in the back of her head
that can see kids fooling around even when
she's not looking.

In school, we were learning about our

environment. "Colfax School is 'going green,'"

Mrs. H. said. "Can someone tell me what that

means?"

Robert Chen raised his hand. "It means we

have to recycle, reduce, and reuse to keep our

earth healthy."

Robert's my best friend. He's really smart,

and he can even spell words backward.

Mrs. H. gave Robert her "smart kid" smile.

"Now who can tell me why we recycle?"

Cookie raised his hand. "So things we

throw away don't go into landfills," he said.

Cookie's my second-best friend. His real

name is Reginald Cook. No one gets too close

to him because he farts.

"Waste is a big problem for our planet,"

Mrs. H. said. "Trash in landfills breaks down

very slowly, and some will take thousands of

years to rot away."

Here's where I bury my trash:

1. Under my bed

2. In the back of my closet

3. Inside my smelly sneakers

Mrs. H. told Cookie that he could be our recycle monitor. "We have small containers in our classroom marked with the recycling symbol," she said. "Your job is to empty them into the larger bins in the hallway."

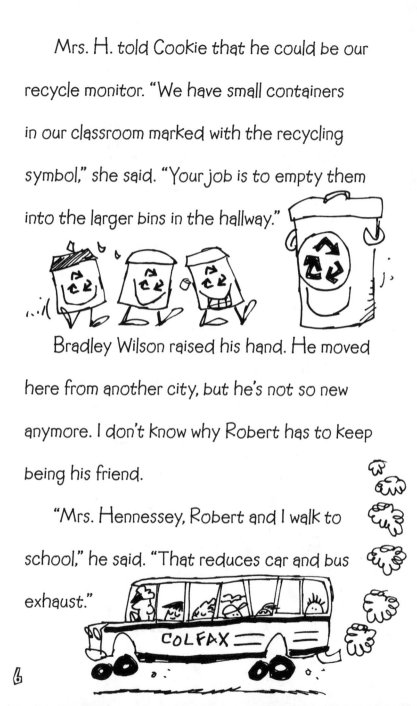

Bradley Wilson raised his hand. He moved here from another city, but he's not so new anymore. I don't know why Robert has to keep being his friend.

"Mrs. Hennessey, Robert and I walk to school," he said. "That reduces car and bus exhaust."

COLFAX

● "Walking is a better choice, and it's good exercise!" Mrs. H. said.

● Mrs. H. picked Bradley to be the energy monitor. His job is to turn out the lights when we leave the classroom.

● Rachel Woolsey said that she reuses plastic milk jugs. "I turn them into bird feeders so they don't end up in a landfill."

● Rachel's our class president. She picked me to be the vice president. I don't do anything, because that's what vice presidents do.

Next, Mrs. H. said we had to write down

ways we can reuse things so they don't get

thrown away.

I tore out a sheet of paper from my

notebook and doodled on the back. That's

how I reuse paper!

Suddenly, Wax Baxter jumped up out of his

seat. "Mrs. Hennessey, Sam's doodling!" he

shouted.

Wax is the biggest tattletale in the third

grade. His real name is Max, but everyone calls him "Wax" because one time we had a contest to see who could pick the most wax from our ears, and he won.

And here's the thing that stinks worse than my burp after I eat a chili dog: Wax's dad is my mom's boyfriend—and he wants to marry her!

"Sam, you can be the paper monitor," Mrs. H. said. "Your job is to collect scrap paper and put it in the recycled-paper bin."

Great! Now I'll have lots of paper to doodle on!

Chapter Two
A Shark Doodle

On Monday, we have assembly. "Walk quietly and stay in line," Mrs. H. said as we followed her to the auditorium.

I like going to assembly because I get to see all the other kids from my school, and we don't have to do schoolwork. **YAY!**

"Class, we'll be sitting here," Mrs. H. said, pointing to the two front rows of seats.

Meghan Diaz and Nicole McDonald sat

on either side of me. They do everything the

same, and they're really annoying.

"We wear hand-me-downs," Meghan said

proudly. "That's how we reuse."

"We're going green!" Nicole added.

"I wear hand-me-downs, too," I said. "My

cousin Ira gave me his T-shirt. He didn't want

it anymore because one time he wore it to

school, and the principal sent him home."

Mrs. Lewis stepped up to the stage and told everyone to be quiet. She's our principal, and I never want to be sent to her office. A sixth grader said there's a shark tank in there. When kids get in trouble, she feeds them to the shark!

"I have an important announcement to make," Mrs. Lewis said.

Great! Maybe she's going to say we can all

go home early.

"Today we have a special guest," she

continued. "Her name is Ms. Thompson, and

she's the director of the Environmental Center.

Let's give her a warm Colfax Elementary School

welcome."

Everyone cheered and clapped really

loudly.

"Good morning, students and teachers!"

Ms. Thompson said. "I'd like to tell you about

our community's Environmental Center. We

have acres of woodland habitats, marshes, and

wetlands. You can walk the nature trails and

see native plants and wildlife. And we offer

classes to learn about conserving our natural

resources. "

WILDLIFE

I jumped out of my seat. "Ms. Thompson,

my grandpa works at the Environmental

Center!" I said.

Mrs. H. shot me a look that meant I shouldn't interrupt the guest speaker. But Ms. Thompson didn't seem to mind. She said they have many wonderful volunteers, just like my grandpa.

For the rest of assembly, we watched a movie about the Environmental Center and how you can go camping there.

When the movie was over, Mrs. Lewis thanked Ms. Thompson for showing us how important the Environmental Center is to our community.

On our way back to class, Wax came up to me. "Your grandpa won't be working at the Environmental Center much longer, Dribble."

"Oh yes, he will, Wax. He has a very important job."

"My dad told me that they're running out of money, and the place might close," he said.

I stopped dead in my tracks. Oh no! If the Environmental Center closes, then someone will come in and cut down all the trees to build a parking lot. And Wax is right—Grandpa will lose his job! **HoNK!!**

"How much do they need, Wax? I've got twelve bucks saved up from my allowance."

"That's not enough, Dribble. They're going to need lots more money," Wax said, shaking his head.

And the only thing I could do was to shake my head, too.

Chapter Three
An itchy Underpants Doodle

The next day in school, Wax and I were

hanging up our coats outside the classroom.

"Dribble, my dad said he still likes your mom.

If they get married, then we'll be brothers."

"That won't happen, Wax. I made my mom

promise she'll never get married."

Here's what I'd rather do than have Wax for a

brother:

1. Eat broccoli every day of my life

2. Get flannel pajamas for Christmas

3. Wear itchy underpants

Then Robert and Bradley came over.

"We're starting an environmental club,"

Robert said. "And I'm going to be the club's

president!"

"That's a great idea! I can be the club's

vice president."

"Sorry, Sam, Brad's already the vice president. But you can be the club doodler and draw our posters."

"I think an environmental club is a dumb idea," Wax said. "All they do is talk about garbage."

"That's not true," Bradley told Wax, who had clearly been eavesdropping on our conversation. "Some clubs plant a garden, and others visit water treatment plants."

When the bell rang, we grabbed our books and hurried into class. Wax ran up to Mrs. H.'s desk.

"Mrs. Hennessey, I think we should start

an environmental club," he said. "We can plant a

garden and visit water treatment plants."

"Mrs. Hennessey . . . ," I started to say.

"Wax copied—"

"I'm talking to Max now, Sam," Mrs. H. said.

"Please don't interrupt."

Mrs. H. told Wax that she liked his

idea. "We can get the whole class involved,"

she said. "Class, how many of you want to

participate in an environmental club?"

Everyone called out, "Me!"

Wax got up from his seat. "Mrs.

Hennessey, since it was my idea, I'd like to be

the club's president."

"It was Robert's idea first!" I called out. "So he should be president."

The class agreed, and Robert got to be the club's president.

"Now let's decide on the goals of the environmental club," Mrs. H. said. "What do we want to accomplish?"

"We can help the Environmental Center because it needs money, and my grandpa works there," I called out.

Mrs. H. said, "The Environmental Center is a great place to learn about our environment, and there are many ways we can help."

Nicole said she thought we should put up

posters to tell people in the community how

much fun it is to have picnics there.

"Our club could volunteer to take people

for walks and show them the wilderness

preserves," Meghan said.

"But, Mrs. H., you don't get it," I called

out. "The Environmental Center needs

money. And if they don't get it, there'll be no

Environmental Center to have picnics at!"

Mrs. H. raised her eyebrows.

"I know!" Robert shouted. "We could have a talent show and give the money we make to the Environmental Center."

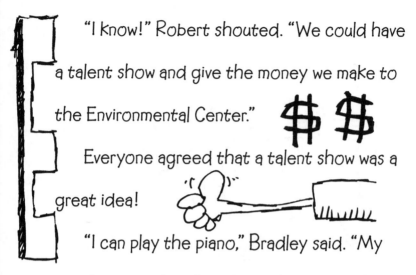

Everyone agreed that a talent show was a great idea!

"I can play the piano," Bradley said. "My teacher said that I'm a musical prodigy. That means you are born with unbelievable natural talent."

Cookie said he could do a comedy act.

Robert said he knew how to break-dance. "My brother taught me how. It's really cool."

Rachel, Meghan, and Nicole said they would perform together. "We can dress up and play musical instruments," Nicole said.

"We'll be a girl band," Meghan added.

"I'll be the leader, since I'm the class president," Rachel said.

Wax said that he had so many talents, he couldn't decide which one to pick.

"Let's have the talent show next Saturday," Mrs. H. said. "That will give everyone time to practice. We'll invite the whole community and open it up to all Colfax Elementary School students who want to participate. We can charge five dollars for admission and sell snacks to raise money. This weekend, ask your parents if they would be willing to help. We'll need as many volunteers as we can get. Also, I'll post a sign-up sheet. Think about what you want to perform, and you can sign up then."

I walked over to Mrs. H.'s desk. "Mrs. Hennessey, what if a kid's only talent is doodling, which can't be performed onstage?

Then how can he be in the show?"

"We all have different talents," Mrs. H. explained. "Some we're better at than others. You'll know in your heart what you were meant to do."

I wasn't quite sure what she meant by that. But I was still glad we were having the talent show. If only I could figure out what I should do!

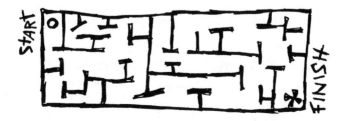

Chapter Four
A Hairy Armpit Doodle

On Wednesday afternoon, Mrs. H.

announced we had library. "Class, as part of

learning about going green, I want you to

read about the effects of pollution on our

environment."

Mrs. Booker is the school librarian. She

was waiting for us as we filed into the library. I

bet she got picked because her name sounds

like the word *book*. My grandpa said our

name is from the cave dwellers, and it means

nincompoop in caveman

words.

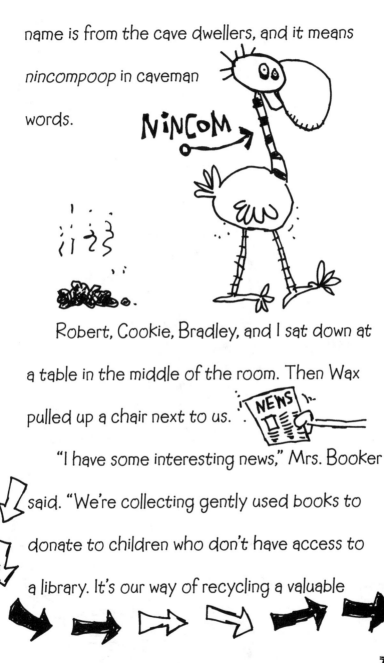

NiNCOM →

Robert, Cookie, Bradley, and I sat down at

a table in the middle of the room. Then Wax

pulled up a chair next to us.

NEWS

"I have some interesting news," Mrs. Booker

said. "We're collecting gently used books to

donate to children who don't have access to

a library. It's our way of recycling a valuable

resource. So if you have any books at home

you would like to donate, please bring them

and place them in this box by Friday."

No way am I giving away my favorite book!

It's a book about people who hold world

records.

Then Mrs. Booker said we could get up

from our seats and use the library's collection

of nonfiction books and the Internet to

research the effects of pollution.

Robert, Cookie, and I walked over to the shelves of books about pollution. "A single cow can belch and fart anywhere from twenty-five to one hundred thirty gallons of methane gas a day. A farm in Vermont converts the cows' gas into electricity," Robert said.

If Cookie turned his farts into electricity, he'd be helping the environment, and we wouldn't have so much pollution!

The library's computers were in the back

of the room. When I got there, they were all

taken. **WAITING...**

Rachel was busy working at her computer.

"I'm almost done," she told me.

I didn't have anything to do while I waited,

so I looked through the box of donated

books. There were books like *How to Fix a*

Toilet and *Grow Your Own Lima Beans.*

Then I found a book I really liked. In the

first chapter of *Juggling for Dummies*, it said

that the first thing you have to learn is how to

stand the right way.

While everyone was busy doing the

assignment, I picked up a hall pass from Mrs.

Booker's desk and went to the bathroom. I

needed some space to practice how to stand

when juggling.

I hoped no one was in the bathroom, but

when I looked under the stall divider, I saw a

pair of giant tennis shoes. They could only

belong to one kid!

Marvin Willis is the biggest kid in the third grade. He has a mustache and hairy armpits.

"Is that you, Marvin?" I called out. "It's me, Sam Dibble."

"Hi, Sam," Marvin grunted. "What're you doing?"

"Our school is having a talent show, and I'm going to juggle in it. But I have to learn how."

"Here's something you can practice with," Marvin said, slipping a stress ball under the divider. "I squeeze it to get strong, so I can smash bricks with my bare hands."

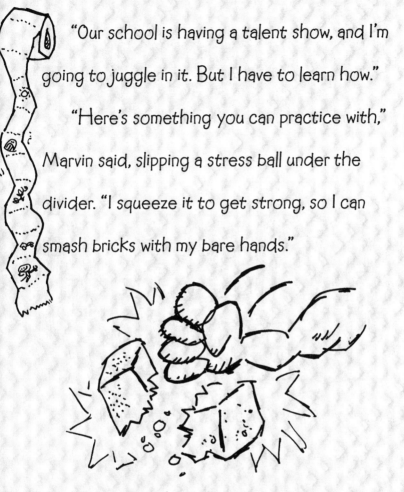

I picked up the ball and tried to remember what the book said about juggling with one ball.

First, I stood with my legs spread apart.

I held the stress ball in one hand and threw

it toward my other hand, but when I tried to

catch it, I missed. *Plop!* The ball fell right into

the toilet.

Gross! I wasn't going to fish the ball out of

the toilet, so I walked out of the stall.

Marvin was now over by the sink, and I

told him what had happened. "You need more

practice," he said. "It takes time to get good."

Just then, Wax came into the bathroom

and headed straight for the stall with the ball

in the toilet!   **UH·OH** ➡

"Don't flush it, Wax!" I shouted.

"Can't hear you, Dribble. What'd you say?"

"I said, DON'T FLUSH THE TOILET!"

But it was too late.

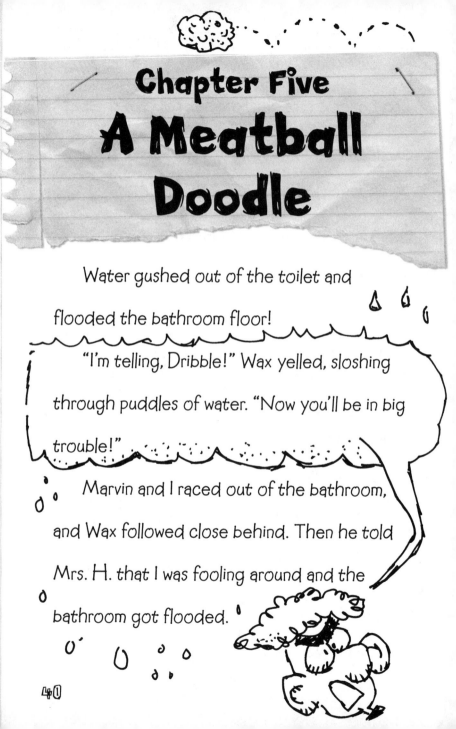

Chapter Five
A Meatball Doodle

Water gushed out of the toilet and flooded the bathroom floor!

"I'm telling, Dribble!" Wax yelled, sloshing through puddles of water. "Now you'll be in big trouble!"

Marvin and I raced out of the bathroom, and Wax followed close behind. Then he told Mrs. H. that I was fooling around and the bathroom got flooded.

Mrs. H. said accidents happen sometimes, and Mr. Penrod would mop up the water, and that next time I shouldn't juggle in the bathroom.

Mr. Penrod is the school custodian. Everyone says that he doesn't like kids because he has to clean up their barf and snotty tissues.

Back in the classroom, Bradley walked over

to my desk. "Wax is mad at you," he said. "His new shoes got wet, and he's telling everyone you did it on purpose."

"It was an accident! I was juggling, and the toilet got plugged up."

Mrs. H. gave me her laser eye and told Bradley to go back to his seat. Then she said, "All right, class, I'd like to know what you learned about pollution and our environment. Sam, why don't you start?"

Wax jumped up out of his seat. "Mrs. Hennessey, Sam didn't even do the assignment. He was too busy reading a book about juggling!"

Wax Baxter should keep his mouth shut

because he makes noise pollution!

DRIVE
TRUCK
THROUGH
HERE

Mrs. H. told Wax to wait his turn. Then

she looked over at me. "Go ahead, Sam," she

said.

It got really quiet in the room. I had to

think about it for a minute. Then I remembered

what Robert had said to Cookie, so I told Mrs.

H. about the cows and the methane gas.

"That's very interesting," Mrs. H. said.

"You made good use of the resources in our library!"

 Bradley whispered something to Robert. And Robert didn't look very happy. Oh well. What did he expect me to do? Get in trouble?

Rachel said that she learned when it rains, the fertilizers farmers use to help crops grow can wash off into waterways and pollute our water.

The bell rang. "Time for lunch," Mrs. H. said. "Please gather your belongings and line up by the door."

All around the lunchroom were bins for recycling plastic bottles and cardboard trays. Another bin was for composting food.

I got in line, and the lunch lady handed me a tray holding two mystery meatballs, slimy spaghetti, slippery sliced peaches, and a carton of milk.

I took my tray over to the table where Robert, Bradley, and Cookie were sitting. Wax sat down with us. "Too bad you can't even juggle one ball, Dribble!" he said, shaking his

head.

"I can juggle two balls, Wax! I read how to

do it in a book."

Wax looked down at my lunch tray. "Okay,

if you can juggle two balls, then let's see you

juggle two meatballs."

The book didn't say anything about

juggling meatballs.

"Don't do it, Sam," Robert warned. "If you

get in trouble, you'll get sent to Mrs. Lewis's

office."

Cookie nodded. "Robert's right, Sam," he

said. Then he farted.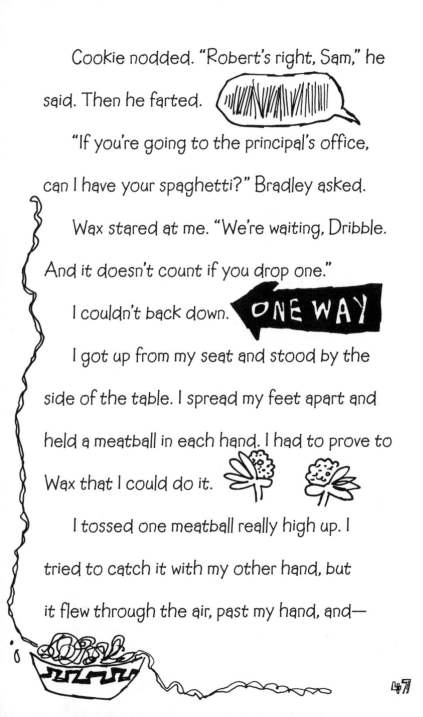

"If you're going to the principal's office,

can I have your spaghetti?" Bradley asked.

Wax stared at me. "We're waiting, Dribble.

And it doesn't count if you drop one."

I couldn't back down. ONE WAY

I got up from my seat and stood by the

side of the table. I spread my feet apart and

held a meatball in each hand. I had to prove to

Wax that I could do it.

I tossed one meatball really high up. I

tried to catch it with my other hand, but

it flew through the air, past my hand, and—

SMACK!— right into Mr. Penrod's head, just

as he walked by.

Mr. Penrod froze. He then reached up and

grabbed the meatball off his head.

"Well, I never!" he said. "I've mopped up

barf and picked up snotty tissues, but this is

the first time I've ever had a meatball on my

head."

Then the most amazing thing happened:

Mr. Penrod started to laugh! And it wasn't

just a little laugh, but a great big "hee-haw!"

I quickly told Mr. Penrod that I was sorry

the meatball had landed on his head.

"Well, keep practicing, Sam," he said. "You'll

get it one of these days."

At recess, I practiced juggling baseballs,

softballs, basketballs, and volleyballs. But every

time, I dropped a ball. I wasn't ever going to get

this whole juggling thing.

Chapter Six
An Earth Day Parade Doodle

The next day, the environmental club made

flyers for the talent show.

"Let me have your attention, everyone,"
Mrs. H. said. "I have some great news. Principal
Lewis has arranged for the performer with the
best act to ride on a float in our town's Earth
Day parade!"

That would be awesome! I wanted to ride
on the float. Last year, our town celebrated
Earth Day with a parade. There were marching
bands, and people rode their bikes in the
street.

But Wax turned to me and said, "Your act doesn't have a chance, Dribble. I'm going to win the talent show and ride on the float."

"We don't know who's going to win," Robert said. "It could be me or even Sam." I gave Robert a high five. Then I asked him if he wanted to hang out after school. "We can go around and put flyers in people's mailboxes."

"I can't," Robert said. "Bradley invited me to his house so we can play video games. He's got a giant sixty-inch, six hundred-hertz plasma HDTV."

"Did Bradley say I could come over, too?"

1 "His mom said he could only have one kid

at a time. Maybe you can go another day."

"You shouldn't play games on that TV," I

warned Robert. "It uses up too much energy. It

isn't good for the environment."

"We're only playing one video game, so it's

not a big deal."

Rachel said that she and Meghan were

going over to Nicole's house. "We're making

programs for the talent show."

I asked Cookie if he wanted to hang out with me. "I can't," he said. "I have to find jokes for my comedy routine."

Wax still wasn't telling what he was doing in the talent show. "I'll announce it when I'm ready," he said. "But everyone will be surprised, especially you, Dribble!"

When I got home, Grandpa was sitting on the couch knitting. "Give me a minute, Sammy-boy," he said. "I might have dropped a stitch."

"One, two, three, four . . . okay, they're all here. Your mom tells me there's going to be a talent show to benefit the Environmental Center, Sammy-boy."

"We're going to raise lots of money, Grandpa, so you can keep your job."

Grandpa put down his knitting. "That's good news, Sammy-boy. It's the best job I've ever had. Be a shame if I lost it."

ANIMAL COSTUMES FOR SALE one used Bear costume: NEEDS WASHING 555-BEAr

Just then, my mom walked into the room.

"Jeff is stopping by," she said, smiling. "We're

making dinner together."

Jeff is Wax's dad. He owns a funeral home,

so he touches dead bodies every day. When

Mr. Baxter sees me, he always wants to shake

my hand. But I tell him I can't because I just

picked a wedgie from my butt.

"He'd better not be bringing Lucy!" I said.
"I have to practice juggling, and she'll get in
the way."

Lucy is Wax's annoying little sister. She has
pigtails that stick out from the sides of her
head and is missing her two front teeth.

But before my mom could say anything,
the doorbell rang. And guess who it was? Mr.
Baxter and Lucy. My really bad day just got
worse!

Chapter Seven
A Lightsaber Doodle

Lucy barged into the hallway. "Hello, Sammy Bibble-Dibble," she said. "I'm doing magic tricks in the talent show. Wax told me you don't have any talent. So I'm picking you to be my assistant!"

"How nice," my mom said with a smile.

Suddenly, the taco I'd eaten for lunch started doing the Mexican hat dance in my stomach.

Lucy tugged on my arm. "Let's go, Sammy

Nibble-Dribble," she said. "We can practice in

your room."

"Look, Lucy, I'm really busy tonight, so I

can't help you with your magic act."

"Daddy, Sam's the meanest boy ever," Lucy

cried. "I want to go home right now!"

My mom took me aside. "Why don't you help Lucy out just for tonight? You can decide later if you want to be in her act."

"No way, Mom! Magicians' assistants are always girls!"

Wax's dad walked over. "I'll make it worth your while," he said with a wink.

I thought about it for a minute. "Okay, but it's just this one time."

My mom and Wax's dad went to the

kitchen to make dinner. Grandpa said he was

going to finish knitting his scarf.

Lucy followed me to my room. "Make sure

you don't touch my shark tooth collection," I

warned her.

"It smells gross in here," Lucy said.

I quickly shoved my dirty gym socks under

my bed. "Tell me what you want me to do, Lucy,

and make it quick. I have to practice juggling

for the talent show."

"I need money to do my first trick," Lucy

said. "You're my assistant, so you have to give

it to me."

I reached into the peanut butter jar I kept

hidden in my closet and handed her a dollar

bill.

"Don't lose it. I'm saving up my money to

buy a lightsaber."

LUKE DIBBLEWALKER

"Ladies and gentleman," Lucy said, waving the dollar in the air. "Watch me turn this dollar bill into two dollars." Then she picked up a pair of scissors and cut my dollar bill in half!

"I can't believe you just did that!" I yelled.

"You don't have to get mad," said Lucy. "My next trick will be better. Watch as I make a candy bar disappear. Does anyone have some candy?"

Since I was the only other person in the

room, I dug into my stash of Halloween candy

and handed Lucy a chocolate bar.

"Thank you, sir," she said. "Now watch

closely as I make this candy bar disappear."

Lucy waved a pretend magic wand. "Tickle,

nickel, sour pickle," she chanted. "Make this

candy disappear!"

"Wait a minute, that's no trick," I shouted. "You just ate my candy bar!" **GONE!**

"Yeah, but I made it disappear. Didn't I, Sammy Piddle-Diddle?"

I couldn't wait to see what dumb trick Lucy was going to do next.

"My next trick is the best one yet," Lucy said. "But I need some string."

"I'm not getting you the string. I helped you out with your other tricks, and now I'm out a dollar and my chocolate bar is gone!"

"Just give me one more chance," Lucy pleaded. "I promise this trick will be really good."

"Okay, but this is the last time I'm helping

you."

I found a ball of string in my desk drawer.

I keep adding to it so I can set the world

record.

Lucy took the ball of string and wrapped it

tightly around me so I couldn't move.

"Fiddle-dee-dee," Lucy sang, dancing

around me. "Get Sammy Dribble free!"

I waited a few minutes, but nothing  happened. "Lucy, untie me!" I yelled. "This magic trick stinks!"

"No!" said Lucy. "You're the rottenest assistant ever, Sam Dibble. And you're fired!"

Then Lucy turned around and marched out of my room!

Chapter Eight
A Humpty Dumpty Doodle

I kept practicing, but juggling was a lot

harder than the book said it would be.

 On Saturday morning, Cookie came over.

"Wax is telling everyone you have two left

hands and that's why you keep dropping things

when you juggle," Cookie said.

"The book said that it's no big deal if sometimes you drop things," I said. "You just say something to distract the audience, then quickly pick it up."

Someone Farted!

"And Wax told me that jugglers wear costumes when they juggle," Cookie said.

"Maybe I'll wear my Halloween costume and call myself Count Jugula," I told Cookie.

"Wax also said that really great jugglers can juggle lots of different things."

For once, Wax was right. I have to challenge myself if I want to have the best act in the talent show. And as much as I want to save the Environmental Center, I want even more to ride on the float in the parade.

"Cookie, let's go into the kitchen, and I'll find something that's difficult to juggle."

There was a bunch of bananas on the kitchen table, but anybody can juggle bananas.

I opened the kitchen cabinets and checked out my mom's good dishes. "Don't even think about it," Cookie said.

Next, I opened the refrigerator and took out three eggs. "Do you think I can juggle these?" I asked.

Before Cookie could answer, I held two eggs in my right hand and one egg in my left hand. Then I tossed all three eggs up in the air.

Just as the eggs hit the floor, my mom walked into the kitchen. "Sam Dibble, what have you done now?" she said. "Look at this mess!"

Then Grandpa walked into the kitchen and

said, "Guess we're having scrambled eggs for

dinner."

My mom made me promise that next time

I practice juggling, I'll use rubber balls. "And do

it in the backyard," she added.

The rest of the weekend I practiced

juggling, but I still couldn't get the hang of it.

On Monday morning, Mrs. H. posted a

sign-up sheet for the talent show. "Write your

act in the space next to your name."

I raced over to the sign-up sheet. Wax

was there ahead of me. "Well, that makes it

official," he said, putting away his pen.

"What's official?" I asked.

"What I'll be doing in the talent show.

Here, see for yourself, Dribble."

"You can't, Wax!" I shouted. "That's what

I'm doing!"

"Too bad, Dribble. There's no rule that says two people can't do the same thing."

Oh no, now I've really got to get good at juggling. Otherwise, Wax will win the talent show!

Chapter Nine
A Toe Fuzz Doodle

The rest of the day, Wax bragged about his juggling act. "My dad hired a professional juggler to teach me some amazing tricks," he said.

Rachel thought that her act with Meghan and Nicole had a chance to win. "Our act is original and it's eco-friendly," she said.

"Our instruments are homemade," Nicole said.

"You'll have to wait for the talent show to find out what they are," Meghan added.

Cookie said he was working on his jokes. "Here's one: Why do elephants have trunks?"

"Because they don't have pockets to put things in," Wax answered. "Everyone knows that joke, and it's not even funny."

Cookie looked miserable. Just like the time he ate a bean burrito and couldn't fart because we were in the library and we had to

be quiet.

X "Okay, here's another joke," Cookie said.

"Why did the banana go to the doctor?"

X "Because it wasn't 'peeling' well. That one's

as old as my toe-fuzz collection, Cookie," Wax

said.

"My mom's taking me to get a tuxedo for

the talent show," Bradley said. "That's what

pianists wear when they perform."

BRADLEY

Robert said he was wearing torn jeans and an old T-shirt for his break-dance routine. "I'm still working on some moves. But I think I have a chance to win."

The talent show was Saturday, and I didn't have much time left to get better than Wax.

When I got home from school, Grandpa told me that Mr. Baxter was visiting. "He and your mom are volunteering to work backstage at the talent show," he said.

"Grandpa, I have to ask you something," I

said. "What if a kid is in the talent show, and he wants to juggle, but he isn't very good. What should he do?"

"This reminds me of my cousin Dunkin' Dibble. He really wanted to play professional basketball."

"Did he do it, Grandpa?" I asked.

"Nope. He was too short. But he made a fortune selling donuts!"

I figured Grandpa was trying to say that if you can't do one thing well, you should try something else.

My mom and Mr. Baxter walked into the room. "Are you ready for the talent show, Sam?" Mr. Baxter said.

"Sort of. Wax told me he's juggling, too."

"I'm sure you'll both be great competitors," Mr. Baxter said.

"Did Mrs. Hennessey give you any homework for tonight?" my mom asked, changing the subject.

"She said we had to write down what we do at home to protect the environment."

"Well, we recycle our garbage, and I try to buy eco-friendly cleaning products."

"I don't flush the toilet," Grandpa said. "That way we save on water."

Here's what I do to help the environment:

1. Compost old Halloween candy

2. Don't take baths or showers

3. Do homework in the dark

DONE!

Mr. Baxter put his arm around my mom. "I'm

cooking dinner for everyone tonight," he said.

"It's chicken with almonds and honey."

"What's that, Baxter?" Grandpa said. "You

say you're the Easter bunny?"

Wax's dad turned to my mom. "Grandpa

Dibble has a great sense of humor," he said.

My mom and Mr. Baxter went into the

kitchen to make dinner, and I went to my room

to finish my homework.

The day wasn't getting any better. First, I found out that Wax is also juggling, and now Mr. Baxter is hanging out with my mom making chicken for dinner—and I don't even like chicken!

When Wax and Lucy showed up for dinner, my mom said that we were like one big, happy family. I think she's wrong about the *happy* part!

Chapter Ten
A Lightbulb Doodle

It was finally Friday, the day before the talent show. In class, Mrs. H. said that many people are concerned the Earth is getting warmer. "We know for sure that gases from burning fossil fuels help trap heat in the atmosphere, and this is one of the many causes of global warming," she said.

"Changes in temperature have an effect on wildlife and are quickly becoming a threat to their survival," she continued.

Here's what I need to survive:

1. Paper and a pencil

2. My superhero pajamas

3. My cat, Fang

4. Takeout pizza

Mrs. H. wrote the words *extinct* and *endangered* on the whiteboard. "Who can tell me what these words mean?" she asked.

Cookie raised his hand. "*Endangered* means that a plant or animal is in trouble, and if they disappear, they're called *extinct*."

"Excellent, Reginald! Now, let's go over to the computer lab, where we can learn more about climate change and global warming."

I like the computer lab because we get to use our own computer and because Miss Garcia, the computer teacher, is really nice.

"Good morning," Miss Garcia said.

"Please take a seat in front of your assigned computer."

My computer was next to Wax's. "Dribble,

my sister said you messed up her magic act.

Now she has to get another assistant."

"Lucy cut my dollar bill in half, ate my candy

bar, and then tied me up!"

"She's just a little kid, Dribble. You should

be nice to her."

"I am being nice, Wax, but I don't want to

be in her magic act."

"Now, let's get to work," Miss Garcia said.

"Use your computer to research the effects

of global warming in the Arctic. Type in words

of global warming in the Arctic. Type in words

such as *melting ice caps* and *rising sea levels.*"

I logged on to my computer. I wanted to

watch a YouTube video of juggling, but the

computer buzzed: *brring, brring, brring.*

Miss Garcia hurried over. "Can I help you,

Sam?" she said. "Remember that certain

Goggle

websites are blocked at school."

"He was looking up things about juggling,"
Wax said. "I saw him do it."

"Sam, please stick to the topic of global

warming," Miss Garcia said. "You can watch

juggling some other time."

When Miss Garcia walked away, I looked

up stuff about polar ice caps. I found a website

with photos that showed how ice caps used to

be big. Pictures taken every few years after it

showed that they got smaller and smaller.

I started thinking about ice caps and webcams and juggling. Miss Garcia told us that the webcam is an example of an input device that feeds images in real time to a computer. "The monitor is an output device," she said. "It takes information and shows it on the computer screen."

Suddenly, I had an idea. I knew just what I could do in the talent show!

Chapter Eleven
A Super Computer Doodle

When computer class was over, I asked Miss Garcia if she could help me with my new idea. "I want to be in the talent show, but I'm having trouble juggling. Wax said that doodling isn't a talent, but I think it is."

"I'd be happy to help you. You have many talents, and doodling is certainly one of them."

I described what I wanted to do, and she told me to stop by the computer lab after

school. "We can work on it together," she said.

"I think it's a wonderful idea!"

On our way back to class, Bradley said that

his dad was buying him a new computer. "It's

way better than the ones we have in school,"

he said.

"Brad, no one really cares about all the

things you have," Robert said. "And maybe

we're getting tired of hearing you brag about

them."

"That goes for me, too!" I said. I was happy about what Robert said to Bradley. But I wouldn't mind getting a new supercomputer, either!

Mrs. H. was waiting for us when we got back to class. "Take your seats, everyone," she said. "I have good news about the talent show. We've already sold one hundred tickets. It's going to be a huge success!"

"Mrs. Hennessey, my mom said to tell you she can be the ticket-taker," Rachel said.

"That's wonderful, Rachel! We'll need all the volunteers we can get."

I had asked Grandpa if he wanted to volunteer, but he said that he had a very important job to do that night.

"According to the sign-up sheet, we have a total of twenty-five acts and twelve volunteers," Mrs. H. said. "Each act will have three minutes to perform."

Bradley raised his hand. "Mrs. Hennessey, what if my piano piece is longer than three minutes?"

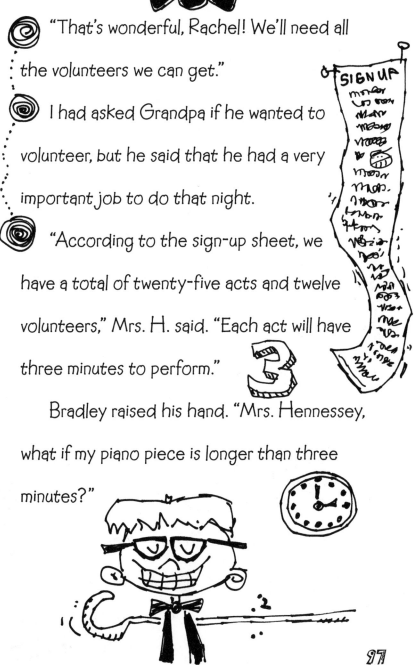

"We can make an exception for some

acts. But I hope you'll try to limit it to a short

piece."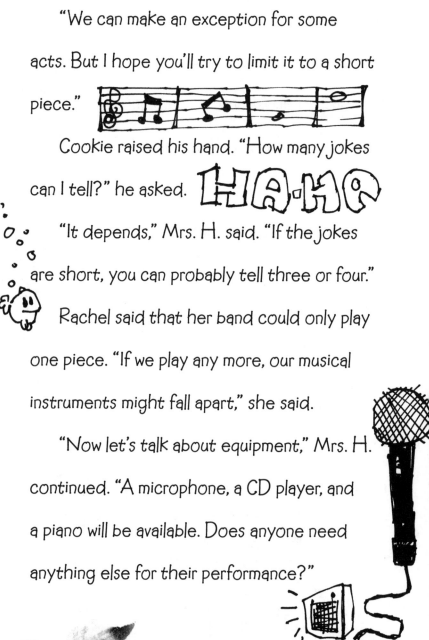

Cookie raised his hand. "How many jokes

can I tell?" he asked.

"It depends," Mrs. H. said. "If the jokes

are short, you can probably tell three or four."

Rachel said that her band could only play

one piece. "If we play any more, our musical

instruments might fall apart," she said.

"Now let's talk about equipment," Mrs. H.

continued. "A microphone, a CD player, and

a piano will be available. Does anyone need

anything else for their performance?"

I raised my hand. "Mrs. Hennessey, I need a computer and a video screen," I said.

"Don't give it to him," Wax called out. "He just wants to juggle things that are hard."

"I'm not juggling them. I need them for my new idea."

"Miss Garcia will be in charge of audio-visual equipment," Mrs. H. said. "And she already told me that she'll provide you with a

computer. She'll help you set up on the night

of the performance, Sam. Now, are there any

other questions?"

No one raised their hands, so Mrs. H.

wished us good luck on our performances. I'm

going to need tons of it to pull off my new act

and beat Wax!

Chapter Twelve
A Two Thumbs-Up Doodle

On the night of the talent show, Grandpa

drove me to school. "Break a leg, Sammy-boy,"

he said, before he dropped me off at the front

entrance.

"Why'd you tell me to break a leg?"

"That's what you say when you want to

wish a performer good luck."

Grandpa said he was parking his car in the

school parking lot. "Then I'll buy my ticket,

101

Sammy-boy, and find a seat in the front row."

My mom had to leave early so she could help out backstage. Mr. Baxter drove her to school in his car.

Mrs. Lewis was waiting by the front door. "If you're a performer, go straight to your classroom," she said. "Your teacher will take you backstage before the show starts."

I walked into my classroom, and Cookie rushed up to me. "What happens if no one

laughs at my jokes?" **BOOOO...**

"Just be yourself and people will laugh."

Then Wax came over. "Dribble, where's

your costume? Did you forget to wear it?"

"My act is so awesome, I don't need a

costume," I told him.

Next, Robert told me he was calling himself

Lil' Rapper Rob. "I'm too cool for school!" he

said.

Rachel, Meghan, and Nicole had on

matching party dresses. Girls do weird things

like that.

"We're carrying our instruments in our

backpacks," Rachel said. "I hope they don't

get crushed."

Nicole bit her nails. "I'm scared to go

onstage in front of all those people," she said.

"Maybe I should have stayed home."

Bradley was wearing a black tuxedo and

white gloves. "I should get a standing ovation

when I'm finished playing," he said.

"Performers, it's time," Mrs. H. announced.

"Follow me to the auditorium. We'll be entering

the stage from the back staircase."

 My mom was backstage when we got there. "How are you doing?" she asked.

"Mom, what if I barf or my pants fall down or I open my mouth to talk and nothing comes out?"

"Take a deep breath. You'll be okay," my mom reassured me. "Everyone gets butterflies before they perform onstage."

Mrs. H. clapped her hands. "Kindergarten performers go onstage first," she said. "Then the rest of the grades will follow in order. The show's about to begin!"

1 I peeked through a crack in the stage curtains. Mrs. Lewis was onstage talking into a microphone.

1 "Good evening, everyone," she said. "I want to welcome you to Colfax Elementary School's first annual talent show."

The audience clapped loudly. "All of our performers have worked hard to present this

show for you tonight," she continued. "They're all winners, but the student with the most outstanding performance will get to ride in the Earth Day parade. And the proceeds from tonight's show will go to the Environmental Center."

I searched the faces in the audience. Then I spotted Miss Garcia. She was sitting in the front row. She must've seen me because she waved and gave me two thumbs-up!

Suddenly, I felt someone pull my shirt. I whipped around to see it was Lucy!

"I'm going first, Sammy Noodle-Doodle," she said.

Mrs. Lewis announced Lucy's name. "Let's give Lucy and her assistant a round of applause."

Then Lucy walked onto the stage. Her assistant was Grandpa!

I watched as Grandpa crawled into a large cardboard box. "Ladies and gentlemen, I will now cut this man in half," Lucy said.

"Don't do it, Lucy," I whispered under my breath. "He's my favorite grandpa!"

When Lucy was done sawing, Grandpa

stepped out of the box. He was still in one

piece! **WHEW**

Lucy and Grandpa took a bow, and the

audience clapped for them. My mom and

Mr. Baxter were waiting for Lucy backstage.

"Great job, Lucy," they both said, patting her

on the back.

The first and second graders went after

the kindergarten kids. And then it was time

for the third graders to take the stage.

I checked the zipper on my pants to make sure it wasn't unzipped. My big chance was almost here, and I couldn't mess it up!

Chapter Thirteen
A Junk Band Doodle

Mrs. Lewis stepped back onto the stage.

"Now, for our next act, we have third grader

Reginald Cook," she said. "He's performing a

comedy routine."

Mrs. Lewis handed Cookie the microphone.

"Hello, ladies and germs," he said.

The audience chuckled, and Cookie

continued: "Here's my first joke: Why did the

rooster run away?"

One of the kids in the audience called out,

"Because he was chicken!"

"Okay . . . here's another one," Cookie

quickly said. "What color is a burp?"

Cookie waited a second. Then he said, "It's

burple!"

No one in the audience laughed. So

Cookie put the microphone up to his butt and

farted, and everyone laughed out loud!

Mrs. Lewis grabbed the microphone

from Cookie. "You can leave the stage now,

Reginald," she said.

The next act was Rachel, Nicole, and

Meghan. Rachel stepped forward and said,

"My name is Rachel Woolsey and this is our junk band."

Then Meghan stepped up to the microphone. "I'm Meghan Diaz. All of our instruments are made from recycled paper-towel tubes, aluminum cans, and cereal boxes."

"I hope you enjoy our song and remember to recycle, reduce, and reuse to keep our Earth healthy and green," Nicole said.

After they finished playing their song, it was Brad's turn to perform. "Bradley Wilson will now play Rimsky-Korsakov's 'The Flight of the Bumblebee,'" Mrs. Lewis said.

The school's piano was in front of the stage. Bradley walked down the steps and took a seat at the piano. No one made a sound as everyone waited for him to start playing.

Bradley sat there and stared at the piano keys. It was like the time I had a big math test and the numbers got all jumbled up in my brain. Mrs. H. said that happens to people sometimes, but next time I'm sitting next to a

kid who's a math genius.

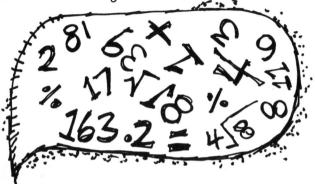

Another minute went by, and I could hear people in the audience saying, "Why isn't he playing?"

I felt kind of bad for Bradley, so I signaled to Robert and we both hurried down the stage steps.

I sat down next to Bradley on the piano bench. "We can play a song together," I whispered. "Do you know 'Chopsticks'?"

Bradley put his hands on the keyboard.

Together, we played a "Chopsticks" duet while

Robert stood in front of the piano and sang a

song he made up about eating with chopsticks.

When we were finished playing, Bradley

and I stood up, faced the audience, and took a

bow.

People cheered and shouted, "Bravo!"

Then Mrs. Lewis said, "Thank you, Bradley,

Robert, and Sam. That was a memorable

performance."

Wax was up next. He juggled three

bananas, five scarves, two Hula-Hoops, and

four bowling pins. And he didn't drop one

thing!

When Wax was finished, the audience

clapped and cheered. Backstage, my mom and

Mr. Baxter hugged each other. *Eww, gross!*

Robert went next. The music was turned

on, and he danced to the beat of a break-

dance song while everyone clapped along.

Then it was my turn. "Now, folks, we have

a very special performance. Sam Dibble, please

take the stage."

I stood up and nodded to Miss Garcia.

She turned off the auditorium lights so all you

could see was the video screen onstage.

"Abra-ca-doodle!"

I said in a loud, booming voice. All of a sudden,

a video animation of a flip book of me juggling

appeared on the video screen!

When the lights came back up, the

audience was on their feet. "That was

Go back to page 100 and flip the pages to see my flip book

awesome!" "Way to go, Sam!" they shouted.

My idea was a success! I took a bow and scooted behind the curtain.

The show was over. I did great, but I didn't win. A second grader, who played the kazoo and sang "The Star-Spangled Banner," won. But Mrs. Lewis said that everyone who participated could march in the parade.

My mom and Mr. Baxter were waiting for me outside the auditorium. "Well done, Sam," my mom said. "I'm very proud of you."

"Group hug," said Mr. Baxter.

Lucy and Wax joined in our group hug.

"You cheated, Dribble," Wax whispered in my

ear. "That wasn't really juggling."

"Can I have another candy bar, Sammy

Piddle-Dibble?" Lucy said.

We all squeezed a little tighter. I had to

get out of there. I felt like I was going to pop!

On Monday, Bradley said he'd give me piano lessons so that we could play a real duet at next year's talent show. Mrs. H. said that between the money we raised and other donations, the Environmental Center would stay open.

Now I'm working on a new doodle. But that's another story.

About the Author

J. Press has taught millions of kids how to doodle. She majored in doodling at Syracuse University and went on to get a master of doodling at the University of Pittsburgh. At home she enjoys spending time doodling with her children and grandchildren. In her spare time she . . . guess what? You're right! She DOODLES!

About the Illustrator

Michael Kline (Mikey) received a doctorate in applied graphite transference from Fizzywiggle Polytechnic and went on to deface (sorry, *illustrate*) over forty books for children, the most notable being one with J. Press involving an ambulance-chasing peanut. The deadly handsome artist calls Wichita, Kansas, home, where he lives with his very understanding wife, Vickie, felines Baxter and Felix, and two sons.